friends
united

Other Friends ⊚ bang on the door ™© titles

friends

Coming Soon

friends again
friends undercover

First published in 2003 in Great Britain
by HarperCollins*Publishers* Ltd.

1 3 5 7 9 8 6 4 2

ISBN: 0-00-715220-5

www.bangonthedoor.com

Text © 2003 HarperCollins*Publishers* Ltd/Lorna Read

Printed and bound in Great Britain by Clays Ltd, St Ives plc.

bang on the door™©

friends
united

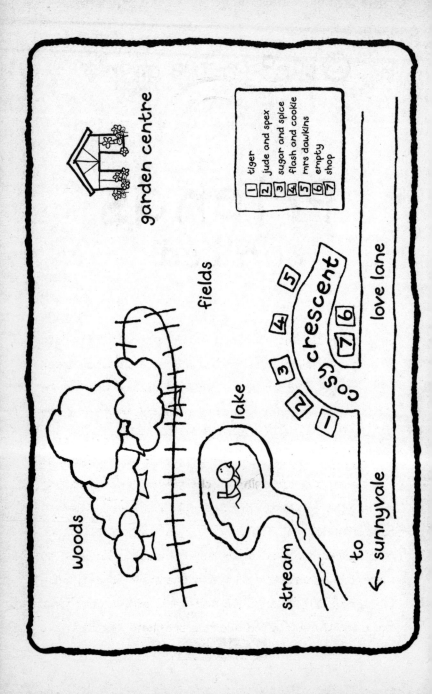

Chapter One

I woke up with an excited feeling, and I couldn't think why. Then I remembered; it was the start of the late May Bank Holiday weekend, which meant a whole week off school! The previous night, I had arranged to meet all my friends at ten o'clock in the morning to go swimming in the big, outdoor pool in Sunnyvale — the town where we live. Of course, we could only go if it was sunny — but, judging by the golden light streaming round the edges of my bedroom curtains, it was a beautiful day!

I quickly gobbled down some muesli and went to meet the others. We all live in the same street, Cosy Crescent. I'm Tiger Cubb and I live at Number One. Spex and Jude McGee are two brothers who live next door at Number Two, twins Sugar and Spice Hart are next to them at Number Three, and brother and sister Flash and Cookie Crumble are at Number Four.

Sunnyvale town centre is about a twenty-minute walk from where we live. You can go down the main road, or over the fields. We chose the fields because it's much nicer. We were all carrying our swimwear and towels and couldn't wait to get to the pool and jump in the lovely, cool water.

"Race you to the baths!" I challenged Jude, when the building was at last in sight.

"OK, Tiger," he agreed.

Everybody shouted, "On your marks, get set, GO!" We sped off and were neck and neck most of the way, until Jude stumbled and I shot ahead of him.

"Beat you!" I yelled, reaching the front steps and punching the air in triumph, advertising my success to the others, who were still catching up with us.

Then I looked up at the signboard outside the building and my heart sank. "Oh, NO!" I wailed. "Just look at this!"

There, in big red letters against a white background, was the ominous word: CLOSED.

"What do they mean, 'closed'? It can't be. It's the holidays. Surely they know that lots of people will want to use the pool?" Spex complained. Of all my friends, he is the serious, deep-thinking one. Not surprisingly, he's the editor of the newspaper we've started, the *Sunnyvale Standard*. We print items of local news, details of sports fixtures, and articles about anything of local interest that we fancy writing about. But mainly we use our paper to cover issues and campaigns that affect our community. It looked as if our latest campaign was right before our eyes!

"Look what it says here." Sugar pointed to a smaller notice pinned to the board beneath the closed sign.

Due to lack of funds for essential repairs and renovations, this swimming pool will be closed until further notice.

I felt anger rising in me. I couldn't let this subject rest. These people, the local council, or whoever was responsible for the pool's upkeep, had no right to do this to us. A lot of people used the pool in the summer, and they would all be upset and annoyed, like us.

"They can't be allowed to get away with this," I said hotly. "There must be something we can do."

"Like what?" asked Flash. He's not known for his bright ideas, but he's a brilliant photographer and always takes his camera with him wherever he goes. One day he hopes to be as famous as his dad, who travels the world taking pictures for newspapers and magazines.

Jude, the tallest among us — and also the oldest by a few weeks (I'm the next oldest) — was standing on tiptoe, squinting at some tiny letters which were painted on the top of the weather-beaten old notice board.

"It says here, 'This pool is managed by Sunnyvale Council Leisure Department. Telephone number...' Anyone got a pen?"

"I have," said Cookie. "I've got a notebook, too." At six years old, she's the youngest of us, but in some ways she's the smartest. She always has an answer for everything.

Jude dictated the telephone number to her and Cookie wrote it down. Then she looked up. "What are we going to do now, if we can't go for a swim?" she asked. Like the rest of us, her face reflected an expression of bitter disappointment. We had all been looking forward to today so much.

"Why don't we all go to the caff in the park and get a drink?" I suggested. "There's a phonebox by the park. Let's ring that number and see if anyone can tell us when the pool is likely to reopen."

That proved to be the daftest idea I'd had so far that day, because, after holding on for ages and ages while the phone rang and rang, we realised that it was Saturday and the council offices were closed.

Gloomily, we bought drinks and clustered around a table in the park. Sugar, whose nickname comes from her sweet tooth, had bought a chocolate-chip muffin and she and Cookie fed a robin with the crumbs. Spice sat with her chin propped on her hands, looking glum. Jude tapped his foot impatiently and drummed his fingers on the table, driving us all mad, and Spex stared off into the distance, seeking inspiration.

I caught Flash's eye. "I have an idea," I said. "While this lot are all sitting here being miserable, why don't you and I walk back to the swimming pool? It won't take a minute."

"OK," he agreed. "Will I need my camera?"

"You bet," I told him, so he pulled it out of his backpack and followed me.

"What do you want me to do?"

"I want you to take a picture of the closed notice in front of the baths. Try to get some clear sky in. It will make the fact that the pool is closed on such a nice day seem even crueller. Then we can publish it in the *Sunnyvale Standard* and write an article about how unfair closing the pool is to all the local people."

Flash snapped away. Then he looked at me, waiting for further orders. While he had been taking his pictures, I had been investigating. The pool was at the edge of the park and I reckoned that, with a bit of help, one or both of us could climb on to the surrounding wall and take a look over.

It was a high wall with spiky iron bits on top, to stop people breaking in and having midnight swims, I supposed. There were no footholds or handy tree branches and I couldn't get up on my own. But I could lift Flash up...

He clambered on to my shoulders and reached for the top of the wall. "Here, Tiger, take my camera in case I drop it," he said, passing it down to me. I slung it round my neck and gripped his ankles again just in time to stop him falling off.

"Done it!" he called triumphantly. "Now what do I do?" He was lying on top of the wall, his legs dangling in the air. I knew he hated heights, so this was very brave of him.

"What can you see?" I asked him.

"Well, there's no water in the pool. The doors are hanging off the changing rooms. It all looks pretty derelict," he reported.

"That's just what we need. Here — take some photos."
I stood on tiptoe and passed his camera up to him.

He took some shots, climbed back down with my help,
and we went back to join the others.

"Where did you two sneak off to?" asked Spice.

"Aha!" I teased her. "We were up to no good!
Actually, Flash climbed up on the wall and took some
pictures of the swimming pool. He says it looks awful in
there. I think it would be great to publish them in the
paper and tell Sunnyvale Council what we think about
this."

"I'll deliver a copy to the council offices personally,"
said Spex grimly. "We don't want to have to wait until
the summer holidays to get a swim!"

I was busy thinking. "There's no point in finishing
the article until we've spoken to the council and found
out when they think the pool might reopen. We need
to quote their reply," I pointed out.

"That means having to wait till Tuesday, when the
staff return after the Bank Holiday," said Spex. "But
we can still get the article started now."

We headed back home full of ideas. As we got back
to Cosy Crescent Cookie suggested we went to her
house for biscuits and a drink before we got started.
We all thought that was a great idea and trooped

round to Number Three. When we got there we found Cookie and Flash's mum with a friend drinking coffee in the back garden.

"Hello kids," said Mrs Crumble. "This is Mary Harris, we used to work together a few years ago."

We all said hello. "How was the swimming?" continued Mrs Crumble, "I bet you could do with a drink and a snack after all that exercise." As she got up to go into the kitchen, we told her about the pool being closed.

"That's funny," said Mary, "I was only talking to a friend of mine who works at the council yesterday and he said that the pool isn't going to reopen, at all."

Chapter Two

"WHAT? Not *ever*?" Cookie's voice was squeaky with disbelief.

We all looked at each other in dismay.

"Are you sure?" asked Mrs Crumble.

"I'm afraid so," said Mary. "But don't take my word for it, why don't you ring my friend, or write to him, and get the whole story. His name is Philip Godfrey and he works in the Leisure Department."

"But why are they closing it?" I demanded hotly. It seemed so unfair.

"Well," Mary explained, "apparently, that particular pool is expensive to maintain. As it's an outdoor one, it's only used during the summer months. This means that the council don't make much money out of it, so they have decided they just can't afford to keep it open. Too many repairs need to be done, so the building is due to be demolished and the site will be put up for sale."

It was the most shocking news that any of us had heard in a long time. Spex was the first to break the gloomy silence that had descended upon us.

"I thought that a leisure facility was... well, just that. A facility. Something for the public to use and enjoy. Surely money shouldn't come into it?"

"Not in an ideal world, no, but the council doesn't have an endless supply of funds." Mary gave a meaningful shrug. "If it doesn't pay, it has to go."

"It's not fair!" Cookie burst out, echoing my thoughts.

"Come on, let's go over to the garage," said Spex. "and get our campaign started."

"What about your snack?" asked Mrs Crumble.

"Thanks Mum," said Flash, but I think we'd better get on to this straight away."

Spex and Jude's garage was where we had set up our newspaper office. Their grandpa used to use it as a workshop, which is why it has an electricity supply. We keep an old kitchen table there, which we use as a work desk – and sometimes as a makeshift table–tennis table! We've managed to inherit some unwanted armchairs and we have a computer, a scanner and a printer on an old side–table, which one of Sugar and Spice's lodgers left behind. We use the computer for doing homework on, and for producing our newspaper.

The only thing we don't have in the garage is a telephone line, so we can't access the Internet, which is a bit of a nuisance. This means that, when we need to do any research, we have to do it on the school computer.

Jude, who is a really good footballer, had to dash off to play in a match that afternoon, so we held the meeting without him. Spex parked himself on the computer chair. It's a bit rickety and squeaks when you turn left or right in it.

"Well," he started. "Are we prepared to have our pool taken away from us without putting up a fight?" Absolutely *not*, we agreed. We'd all been going there for as long as we could remember, and some of us had parents, and even grandparents, who had been swimming there every summer for decades. We guessed they wouldn't be too happy about the pool's closure, either.

"Right, then. Let's think of a headline," he said.

We all pitched in with various suggestions, but it was Flash who came up with the best idea. "How's this? 'Splash, Bang, Wallop! Sunnyvale Council dives into trouble by closing outdoor pool'," he said.

"Wow! Say that again, Flash," said Spex admiringly.

Flash looked bemused. "I don't know if I can remember it. It was only meant as a joke," he said shyly.

Luckily, we all remembered it for him.

"If we're going to have a Save Our Pool campaign, we could call it SOP for short, as in sopping wet!" I suggested.

The others liked my idea and we thought we might even make some badges. Then Spice mentioned something that was troubling me, too. "What exactly are we going to *do* to save the pool? Writing about it isn't enough. We need to suggest something that the residents of Sunnyvale can do to help..."

"Well, like us, they'll all be writing to the council, won't they, and telling them they want the pool open again?" said Flash.

"Will that be enough?" Sugar enquired.

"What if we ask everyone to donate money to a SOP fund?" Spex suggested.

"You need to set a fund up properly, and open a

bank account for it. We'd need the help of the Oldies for that," I reminded him. The Oldies was what we called our parents and all the older residents of Cosy Crescent.

"Oh, we don't want to involve *them!*" said Spice.

"We've got to. The Oldies want the pool to reopen as much as we do. Anyway, it's their generation that has all the money to donate," I pointed out.

We decided we couldn't simply ask for donations, because we probably wouldn't raise enough. Certainly not the thousands of pounds that we needed. We thought about asking swimwear companies to sponsor our pool and decided to write to them and send them a copy of our article. We also decided to approach the various shops and businesses in Sunnyvale, to see if they were interested in paying any money towards the repairs.

By the end of the afternoon, all we had managed to do was draft a letter to Mr Godfrey at the council. We all felt dispirited. Spice and I started a game of table tennis, playing against Flash and Sugar. Cookie went off to post the letter in the box at the end of Cosy Crescent. Meanwhile, Spex sat staring moodily at the computer screen and kicking his foot against his chair.

Amid the noises of the game, I heard him mutter, "What we need is something that unites everyone. Something we could all do together. Something people would enjoy. Hmm... Oh, I don't know." He gave the chair another savage kick.

"Out! We've won!" shouted Sugar.

"You could have hit that easily, Tiger," Spice grumbled at me.

"Sorry," I replied. "I was too busy thinking..."

"What about?" Spex wanted to know.

"Promise you won't laugh?"

"I won't," he promised.

"Well, how about putting on a charity concert, like the ones the pop stars do to raise funds for charity?" I said.

An excited babble broke out.

"That would be brilliant," said Spex. "But I don't see how we could do it. We don't know any pop stars or musicians."

"My dad does," I reminded him. Dad used to play in a band with his mates and knows loads of other musicians.

"Do you think he'd help us?" asked Sugar.

"I'm sure he would," I replied. "But must we ask him? It would be much better if we could arrange the whole thing by ourselves."

Everyone agreed with me.

Spice said, "Let's see if Cookie's back yet. She ought to be in on this."

Flash went to fetch her.

"Right. Let's get to work," Spex said, as soon as they were back.

He grabbed a large sheet of paper. Taking a thick, red, felt-tip pen, he wrote SOP at the top of the page. "What are we going to need?"

"Posters," said Spice.

"Leaflets," added Flash.

"Tickets to sell." That was Cookie.

My own contribution was, "Let's ring the local radio station. They are always interested in charity events."

"We need to contact singers and musicians, to see if anyone will perform for us for free. How are we going to do that?" asked Sugar.

"We could try the Internet," Spex suggested. "A lot of them have their own websites."

"We only need one famous person to agree to appear, and we'd got it made. Everybody will want to come and watch and make a donation to our fund," Spex pointed out.

"What fund?" Suddenly, another person was standing in the doorway.

"Oh, there you are, Jude! We've got it all organised. We're going to put on a charity event to raise money to Save Our Pool!" Spex told his brother proudly.

"A charity football match? That's great! Can I play?" Jude was positively jumping with enthusiasm.

"No, Jude. Not a football match, a concert," I informed him.

"A *concert*? You must joking!" Jude exclaimed. "Everybody does charity concerts. We need something different. A charity football match is just the thing." He paused, and gazed round at us all. "If we make it a charity match, I'll do all I can to help organise it. I do have a few contacts, you know," he said importantly. "But if you insist on a concert, then sorry, I don't want anything to do with it. You're on your own."

And he walked out, leaving us all gaping.

Chapter Three

We Friends had had disagreements before, but never like this. We were all shocked that Jude could be so unhelpful. He has so much energy and is usually so keen to pitch in and do whatever he can to help put our ideas into action.

"Take no notice of him. His team probably lost their match this afternoon," said Spex.

"I think he meant it," said Flash dolefully.

"Look, I know my brother better than anyone. Even if he did mean it, I'll talk him round, so don't worry. Now, let's finish this list," insisted Spex.

Nobody wanted to. Jude's outburst had dampened our spirits, so we all drifted off home, with a weak kind of arrangement to meet again tomorrow.

By the time I arrived at the garage at just past eleven the next morning, Spex was already working hard.

"Hiya," I greeted him. "Did you manage to talk your brother round?"

"No," he replied. "He stuck his headphones on and wouldn't listen."

"Why didn't you try talking to him again at bedtime?"

"He went to sleep with his headphones on, too! Anyway, take a look at this and tell me what you think." He ripped a sheet of paper out of the printer and passed it to me.

It read: *Come to the INTERNATIONAL STAR CONCERT and raise funds to keep Sunnyvale's outdoor swimming pool open. Admission by donation. For information, please ring...* He had added his own mobile phone number.

I looked up. "Er... how do you know we'll find any international stars? And don't you need to put a date in?"

"We can advertise the date as soon as we've found a star to appear." Spex was all smiles.

"Well, I wouldn't distribute this too soon, or else you'll be inundated with calls and won't have any information to give anyone," I pointed out.

Spex's smile faded. "You're so practical, Tiger," he complained. "It ruins my creativity. Oh, how I wish this computer was linked up to the Internet. I need to start work on this straight away."

"There's always the Internet caff in the town centre," I reminded him.

His face brightened. "What a great idea! Do you think it'll be open on a Bank Holiday?"

"Bound to be," I said.

"Let's go see." Spex jumped up and started scribbling something on a note, which he then stuck to the garage door.

The message, obviously aimed at the rest of our friends, read:

Tiger & Spex gone to Sunnyvale. C U L8R.

We told the Oldies where we were going, then set off across the fields. It was a lovely day and I kept asking Spex to slow down so that I could watch a bird, or look at a flower.

He got really impatient with me. "Tiger, come *on!* This is urgent business. You can study nature any time."

Finally, we reached the caff and started our search. We made quite good progress, finding singers' and bands' websites and, where possible, emailing them to invite them to perform at our concert. In each case, we told them what it was in aid of, and gave Spex's mobile phone number.

By the time our hour's computer use was up, we had contacted twenty-three different acts about our charity event, although we usually had to leave our messages on their fan club site, and hope that they would be passed on.

"I never realised what hard work it was, trying to organise a concert," I said.

"Oh, it's not too bad, really. Once we've got some people to appear, the rest will be a piece of cake," Spex assured me, as we sipped cold drinks at a table outside. His words made me hungry, and forced me to go back inside and buy a blueberry muffin!

"I wonder how many people will come?" I mused as I munched. "If a thousand people came and they all donated five pounds, that would be five thousand pounds. Surely that will be enough to do up the pool?"

Spex laughed. "I don't think so," he replied, crushing my hopes. "I imagine it would take a lot more than that to make the pool fit for use again."

I felt my heart sink. "How much more?" I asked weakly.

"Well, I'm no expert, but I reckon it could be at least twenty-five thousand pounds, perhaps more."

"No. You've got to be wrong," I insisted. "No repairs could cost that much."

It looked as if our goal was climbing impossibly out of reach. There was no way we could rely on thousands of people coming to our local concert...

...and that was when my heart sank. For there was something terribly important that we hadn't even thought of!

"Spex," I said. "Where are we going to *hold* this international concert of ours?"

That afternoon, the entire lot of us sat gloomily inside the garage. The sun may have been shining outside, but inside we were utterly miserable. How could we put on a concert if we had nowhere to hold it? None of us had been able to come up with a single suggestion. It looked as if we would have to drop any idea of reopening the swimming pool. Only Jude seemed to be in good spirits.

"Well, maybe we should organise a charity football match after all," he said eventually. "You don't need a concert hall for a football match, all you need is a pitch."

"You know, you might have a point there, Jude," Spex said. "Perhaps it *would* be easier to put on a charity match than a concert."

"Great," said Jude, leaping up. "Now, let's start organising it. I'll ring Mr Queen tomorrow..." Mr Queen was the manager and coach of Sunnyvale Albion, "...and he can put the word around and see who he can get to play for us."

Flash was beginning to look interested. "Who will the superstar team play?"

"Who do you think?" replied Jude. "Us, of course! Well, us with a little help from Sunnyvale Juniors."

"Yeah! Great!" Flash said enthusiastically. "I can't wait to start training."

"And another thing," Jude continued. "A lot of the Sunnyvale Albion team live round here. They all know the pool and will want to help. You can't expect some pop star from London to be interested in helping a tiny town like Sunnyvale keep its swimming pool open," he said.

I knew he was right, but I still couldn't give up on the idea of a concert. I muttered something about having to go home and made a quick exit from the meeting. I knew exactly what I was going to do about it, even if I had to do it alone...

Chapter Four

As I walked glumly down the road, my hands stuffed in my pockets, my toes scuffing the dust, I heard footsteps and turned to find Cookie running after me.

"Tiger! Don't go," she said breathlessly. "I know how you feel. I'd much rather have a concert, too."

"I'm going to find Dad. Come with me," I invited her. "Music's his big thing. He's been to lots of concerts. Maybe he can think of something..."

My father was in the back garden. He had spread newspapers over the grass and his bicycle was lying on them on its side while he sprayed it bright red. "I want to see if a change of colour will make it go faster," he explained.

"Told you I had a mad dad," I whispered to Cookie. "Got a minute?" I asked him.

"Sure. I can't spray the other side till this one's dry. Now, what's this all about? You two look very serious..."

"We are." I told him about my charity concert idea, and how it had been dropped because we couldn't think of a venue for it.

"Why do you need one? What's wrong with holding it in the open air? Maybe we could turn it into an annual event, like the Reading or Glastonbury rock festivals, and release albums from it..." Dad was off again.

I stopped him in mid-fantasy. "Dad, where do you think we could hold it?"

"Ask Mrs Dawkins if it's all right to use her field. I'm sure she'd say yes. I'll rustle up some of my old band members and we'll sort the PA and stage out and even play for you. That should raise a few bob for your fund..."

I hated to point out one hard fact, but I had to say it. "Sorry, Dad, but you're not exactly an international superstar, and that's what we need. Let's see who responds to Spex's emails first," I said. Then, because he looked so disappointed, I promised, "You can be the warm-up act." He seemed quite happy with that.

"Come on, Cookie. Let's go and see Mrs D.," I said. Mrs Dawkins is an old lady who lives at Number Five, she owns the fields at the back of Cosy Crescent. Since Cookie and I had been gone, it was obvious that everyone had been talking about us. Now, as we walked back into the garage, they all fell silent, and stared.

I looked at Jude. "OK. Let's have your charity football match," I said, "but let's have a concert, too. An open-air one. We've just been to see Mrs Dawkins and she says we can use the field. We can have the match in the afternoon at the Sunnyvale Albion grounds, and the concert in the early evening. We can make a whole day of it. Well? What do you think?"

I felt so proud when everyone said that it was a great idea. "The more fundraising events we have, the merrier," Spex confirmed. "We could have stalls in the crescent, too. Snacks, some of your mum's cakes, Tiger, and maybe a jumble sale..."

"We've got a whole house full of jumble," Sugar said.

"Let's go and see Dad!" continued Spice and off they went, while Spex opened a fresh page on the computer and began typing furiously.

Jude, Flash, Cookie and I started discussing the advertising side, the posters and flyers, and the people we should contact.

"Which of my photos are you going to use on the poster?" Flash wanted to know.

"Or shall we use a painting?" Cookie added.

"I think we should use both," I said. "A photograph will look professional for our flyers but one of your nice bright pictures on a poster will really attract attention."

When Sugar and Spice came back, Sugar was carrying a big book. "Look what Dad found!" she told us proudly. "It's called *A Century of Sunnyvale*. It's got some fantastic pictures in it. Here's an old concert poster from a show they put on in Sunnyvale Town Hall in 1908. Look! Wouldn't it make a great poster for us, too?"

"I think we should reproduce the old poster on the press release," Spex said, glancing up from the screen.

"Press release?" I queried.

"Of course!" he replied. "We need something professional-looking to send to the local radio and TV stations and the newspapers. We want them to mention the event because that will attract more people..."

"...and more people means more money!" Jude finished cheerfully. "By the way, had any responses to your emails yet, Spex?"

"Nothing..." Spex shook his head.

"Oh well, it's early days yet. I don't suppose we're going to hold our fundraising day for... well, a month, at least!" I said.

"I think that should be our deadline, otherwise there isn't a chance of the council getting the pool repaired and open by July or August."

Spex's words made me think. We had far less time than I'd realised. We really had no idea about how long the repairs would take. And we didn't want to ask the council, for fear they would squash the idea flat, before we had even had a chance to raise any support from all the other Sunnyvale swimmers!

We went back home to ask our families what they could do to help. After we'd all eaten our evening meal, we met up at the garage again to compare notes. Spice was missing, but Sugar appeared, bursting with enthusiasm about something. "Guess what?" she said eagerly. "You know our lodger, Holly Hodge? She can do face painting. Look what she's done to Spice!"

Spice popped her head round the door and we all gasped, because were looking not at a human being, but at a zebra! Holly had even made a black mane out of strips of paper pinned to Spice's hair. It was terrific!

"Face painting," muttered Spex, writing it down. "Tell Holly we'll definitely be wanting that. Anything else?"

"Dad's got plenty of bric-a-brac," said the zebra – Spice, I mean!

"Mum said she'll make cakes and donate some of her pots of jam and chutney," I said. "By the way, Dad and his band are rehearsing already. You should hear the racket!" The bish-bang of drums and cymbals, and the twanging of guitar strings could be head echoing down the road from our attic.

"Our mum and grandma say it's a good opportunity to spring-clean their wardrobes and chuck out lots of old clothes, so we can have a second-hand clothes stall, too," Jude told us.

"How about Flash and Cookie?" asked Spex, looking up from his list-writing. "Any ideas?"

Flash blushed, looked down and shuffled his feet. Uh-oh, I thought. Something's brewing. He's always shy about coming forward, but, finally, he looked up again, gulped, and suggested, "Cookie thought we could have an art stall. I could sell some of my photographs, or take pictures of people if they'd like me to, and she could sell paintings."

"That's a lovely idea!" I said enthusiastically.

Everyone else agreed and Flash looked very relieved. "I thought you might say 'no'," he admitted.

Jude looked surprised. "Why should we say that?"

"I thought you might think I wasn't good enough..."

"Oh Flash, don't be silly. You've taken some brilliant photographs!" Spice assured him. "And lots of people will want photographs of themselves taken with the football stars."

"Or the music stars," I added, staring at Spex's mobile. *Come on, ring*, I willed it.

Then I nearly fell off my chair when, all of a sudden, it did!

Chapter Five

"Who is it?"

"Come on, Spex, tell us!"

"Sssh! Let's listen to what he's saying..."

Everyone was falling over themselves to find out which pop superstar could be talking to Spex. All he was saying was, "Yes... yes," but excitement was bubbling up inside me. He wasn't saying "no", so it sounded like good news!

At last he came off the line. We all waited expectantly but, instead of telling us who he had been speaking to, he started to tidy up his pens and floppy disks, and switch off the computer equipment.

Jude grabbed his brother's shoulder: "Come on, put us out of our misery. Who rang you?" he demanded.

Spex looked round and blinked owlishly, before pushing his glasses back up his nose. "Only Mum, wanting to remind us that it's getting late and Cookie should be in bed," he said.

We all groaned. The sense of disappointment was tremendous. I glanced at my watch. It was almost nine o'clock

"Just before we pack up, could you do one thing for us?" Spex asked Jude. "Could you ring Mr Queen now? The sooner we know if he can get any football stars to donate their services, the sooner we'll know where we are with this whole charity idea."

Jude looked doubtful. "I don't really like to ring him on a Bank Holiday," he said.

"Well, we can't wait till Tuesday," Spice said sharply.

"You're right," Jude agreed. "Let's go over to our house and I'll call him.

We all squashed into the McGee's hallway and waited in suspense while Jude dialled the number. Mr Queen answered immediately and Jude outlined our idea. Watching Jude's face, I could see him beginning to grin.

"I think he's got someone!" Flash whispered.

Flash was right. "He loved it!" Jude announced, replacing the receiver. "He says he knows that Kev

Healey and Scott McLeonard are free next Saturday, because there are no matches." Kev and Scott are the star players of Sunnyvale Albion. "He'll check with them but he feels sure they'll be only to pleased to do it. And guess what?" Jude grinned even more broadly. "He thinks he might be able to talk Christy Donovan into it, too!"

Christy is an ex-Sunnyvale player who now plays for one of the UK's biggest teams.

"Wow!" Flash cried, jumping up and down. "Christy Donovan! I must get his autograph!"

Everyone was talking excitedly, except me. A very serious fact had registered in my brain with a horrific clang. "Jude, did you say *next* Saturday?" I queried.

"I sure did!" Jude confirmed.

"Well, you know what this means," I said. "We've got less than a week to organise both the match and the concert. How on *earth* are we going to do it?"

My panic infected the others, as there were gasps of, "Oh no!" and pale faces all round.

Cookie had tears in her eyes. "It's impossible," she said miserably.

Sugar put an arm round her. "Cookie's right. Perhaps we're being too ambitious about the whole thing."

"No!" Spex and I said simultaneously.

"No way!" Jude joined in.

"Anyway, we can't stop now. I've already rung the radio station news office and left a message on their answering machine telling them about the Save Our Pool campaign," said Spex. "You've *what*?" exclaimed Spice.

"We agreed to go ahead with publicity at the last meeting" Spex glanced at his watch. "It's late. Let's sleep on it," he suggested.

I didn't sleep a wink that Sunday night. My mind was racing. The whole event rested on two crucial things, and they were whether or not we could muster up two football teams in time, and whether or not we could find a singer or band worthy of being called "international"!

Then I realised that there was a third thing, too: could we distribute all our leaflets and advertising material in time to let enough people know about it?

And then a fourth thing dawned on me. We hadn't found a football pitch yet! Perhaps the teams could play on Sunnyvale Albion's pitch. Jude had forgotten to ask Mr Queen, but I would remind him in the morning. However, until we had the location of the star-studded match sorted out, we couldn't print our leaflets and really start the publicity-ball rolling. Oh, it was all too much...

I had a stomachache in the morning and couldn't eat any breakfast. Mum was worried that I might be coming down with something, and didn't want me to go out, but I managed to persuade her that it was just nerves.

"Maybe you've bitten off more than you can chew," Mum said. "This would be a lot for a grown-up to take on, let alone a bunch of kids!"

I tightened my lips. "We'll do it!" I told her fiercely.

"Well, if you must go out, would you mind taking this round to the Harts' house for me?" she asked, and handed me a carrier bag with some freshly dug potatoes and some wrinkly looking onions in it.

Mum had an agreement with Sugar and Spice's dad. She gave them some of her spare produce from our allotment and greenhouse, in return for our use of the computer. Mr Hart had to stayed home to look after the twins, so he didn't work. Apart from benefits, he relied on a tiny income from taking in a lodger or two. But he always chose the wrong ones, who did a moonlit flit, or gave him a hard-luck story to avoid paying their rent. Holly Hodge, his current lodger, kept the house clean and tidy and did some cooking in lieu of rent, so at least she earned her keep. Apparently she wanted to be a poet, but none of us had ever read anything she had written. We had funny feeling that it was all in her head, rather than on paper!

On my way to the Harts' I bumped into Flash and Cookie, who were going for a walk. "We'll be back soon," they promised. "See you in the garage."

Mr Hart opened the door to me and took the bag. "Thank your mum for me, won't you?" he said.

Spice came down the stairs, wearing denim dungarees with a big green patch on the pocket. Sugar always wears a yellow patch on her clothes. That's how people can tell the twins apart. Sometimes they play a trick on everyone by wearing each other's clothes. That's really funny. Sooner or later, they give the game away by getting the giggles. Of course, you can tell the difference between them if you know them as well as I do. Sugar is the dreamy, artistic one, and Spice is a bit more outgoing. Give them both a pencil and it's Sugar who draws the best pictures.

"Coming to the garage?" I asked Spice. She went to get Sugar.

When we got there, the garage was locked up.

"That's funny," I said, puzzled. "It's not like Spex not to be here first..."

"Perhaps he's overslept," Sugar suggested.

Then we heard the sound of a large vehicle turning into Cosy Crescent. It was an ambulance. A shiver went down my spine.

"Oh, no!" Spice cried. Sugar went quite pale.

The ambulance came to a halt right by where we were standing. A paramedic got out and knocked on the door of Number Two, the McGee's house.

"I can't look," Sugar said, and ran back to her house. Spice ran after her, leaving me alone on the pavement.

My mother appeared in our doorway. "Come in, Tiger. Don't get in the way," she told me.

Reluctantly, I obeyed, though I was desperate to find out who in the McGee household had been taken ill. Perhaps Spex or Jude had developed appendicitis in the night! Another grim thought struck me, too. If one of the McGees had been taken ill and the family had to spend most of their time at the hospital, that would mean the end of our SOP campaign. We couldn't carry on without Spex, and we needed Jude's help with organising the football match. I heaved a deep, deep sigh. Right now, it looked as if the success of the Save Our Pool campaign was hanging by a thread...

Chapter Six

All kinds of horrible thoughts were going round my head. I was so worried about the McGees, my throat choked up with tears. "I... I'm going round to see Sugar and Spice," I said in a muffled voice, and fled up the street.

The twins had their noses pressed to the front window, but they pulled themselves away when I walked into the lounge.

I flung myself on to the sofa and burst out crying. I'm not usually this weak, but right then I felt completely overwhelmed — so much was going wrong all at the same time. To make things worse, we didn't know which McGee had been taken to hospital. Sugar and Spice started to sniff, too, and all three of us huddled together on the sofa.

We didn't hear the bell or the door, but suddenly, there was Holly, the Harts' lodger, ushering someone into the room. It was Jude. We stopped crying as soon as we saw him, and held our breath, wondering what bad news he was about to give us.

"It — it's not Spex, is it?" whispered Sugar.

"What?" Jude looked completely blank for a moment. "Oh, you mean the ambulance?" He burst out laughing. I frowned. What could possibly be funny about an ambulance? "I suppose you thought someone was ill..." Jude was still chuckling away to himself.

"Well, of course we did!" I said sternly.

Jude struck a pose. "Fear not, Tiger Cubb," he boomed, like an actor. "The driver's a friend of Mum's. She was off duty so she popped in for a coffee and a chat. We're all fine!"

I felt so relieved!

"I've come to tell you three that Spex is waiting for you," Jude went on. "He's got an idea about how we can get round the difficulty of not knowing who's going be singing at our concert."

We called for Cookie and Flash. "Ah, Flash. Just the person!" Spex announced as we entered the garage.

"Who, me?" Flash enquired, pointing at himself and giving a goofy grin.

43

"Yes, you!" we all chorused.

"I've got a job for you," Spex told him. "I'd like you to take a publicity photograph of Tiger's dad and his band."

"Brilliant!" Flash exclaimed.

"When are they going to be rehearsing, so that Flash can take the picture?" asked Spex.

"Listen," I said, flinging open the garage door. *Bash...twiddle...plink-plunk...kerash!* "You'll catch them right now. What's this idea that Jude mentioned?"

"We could say that your dad's band will be playing, then build up people's excitement adding by saying that they'll be supporting some Mystery International Guest Stars. That gets round having to name names on the publicity leaflet."

We all thought it was a great idea.

"What's the name of your dad's band?" Spex enquired.

"Haven't a clue. I don't think he's thought of one yet," I replied.

"Well, please ask him to think of one quickly," said Spex. "I need to put it in print today!"

Dad and his musician friends were in our spare room, which is where Dad keeps his drum kit. They were making so much noise that they didn't hear me knocking on the door. In the end, I pushed it open and burst in on them, while Flash lurched after me, strung about with camera equipment. He had brought a tripod with him, and a collapsible umbrella-thing belonging to his father. I had no idea what it was for, but I felt sure Flash would know.

They saw us, but didn't stop playing. They were quite good, actually. When they had finished the number, they stopped and said hello.

"What's all this?" asked Dad.

"We'd like to take a publicity photograph of the band," I said. "And we need to know what name you're going to call yourselves."

"Name?" Dad screwed up his face comically. "I don't think we've thought of one. You're right, we'll need one, won't we? How about *The Wrinklies*?"

Flash and I thought it was funny, but the rest of the band reckoned it was too insulting. Various other names were suggested, then dismissed, amidst hoots of laughter. We were getting nowhere at all.

In the end, I said, "Let's get on with the photos, and think of a name later. Where do you suggest taking it, Flash? Here, with the instruments, or in the garden?"

"I'll try a few in here," said Flash, "though it's a bit

cramped and I mightn't be able to get far enough away for a decent group shot."

He set up his powerful light, then unfolded the big silver umbrella, which he said was called a paraflash and reflected light on to the subject. By standing on the stairs and shooting through the open door, he managed to fit everybody in.

"Let's do some in the garden, too, in case these don't come out very well," he suggested.

While the band members were looning around, sticking flowers in their teeth and pretending to hit each other over the head with guitars, I went to talk to Mum. But the bass guitarist, a red-haired, ginger-bearded man called Tim, interrupted us.

"Hey, Tiger! I think we've decided on a name. What do you say to us getting inspiration from your name and calling the band *The Stripes*, as in tiger stripes?"

I grinned and told them that it was fine by me!

Flash packed up his photographic gear and I helped him carry it back to his house. On the way back to the garage, we met Jude coming out, looking really happy.

"I'm off to meet Mr Queen at the Sunnyvale Albion ground. We're going to talk over arrangements for next Saturday. Want to come?" he asked us.

I shook my head, but Flash jumped at the chance, and went to ask his mum if it was all right to go with Jude. Meanwhile, I carried on into the garage. It was a hive of activity. Cookie, helped by Sugar, was busy painting pictures, trying to decide which one was best for the poster, while Spice checked the newspaper article that Spex had just finished.

"We must get this issue of the *Sunnyvale Standard* printed out tonight, then we can start distributing it tomorrow. That will give people four days' notice. It's not long, but it's the best we can do. We need to splash the posters all over town."

"*Splash!* Ha, ha!" laughed Sugar.

Spex frowned. "As I was saying," he continued, in a brisk, businesslike tone, "we need to get the posters up, get the press releases out to the local radio and TV stations and that journalist we know on the daily paper, leave stacks of flyers in places like the library and the supermarket — maybe even stick some through people's doors. There's loads to do."

"Any phone calls from international stars yet?" I enquired hopefully.

Spex's frown deepened and he shook his head.

"Never mind, we've definitely got *The Stripes*, and

they're really good!" I told him, explaining that was the name Dad's band had picked.

Spex looked a bit happier. "We've got them, we've got some footballers... Yes, it's slowly coming together," he said. "I've decided it would be best not to charge an entrance fee. We'll get more people along if we say that, as it's a fundraiser, the entrance fee is a donation to the SOP fund. Then people can pay whatever they can afford."

"Good idea," I said. "Need any help with the paper?"

"Yes. You can staple," he said.

Stapling the news sheets together was the worst job and we normally all quibbled about who did it the last time, in order to try and wriggle out of it. But this time I was glad to be of assistance. We had two staplers, so, once Spex had printed it out, Sugar or Spice could help, too.

I was looking over Spex's shoulder as he typed in the information about Dad's band, when he remembered something with a jump. "Flash's film won't be developed in time for us to go to press. Have you got any snaps of your dad playing the drums?"

I laughed. "I'm sure I can find something," I promised, and dashed off home.

Dad produced an old suitcase covered in stickers

bearing the names of old rock and folk bands I'd never heard of. He pulled out a photograph and handed it to me.

I stared at it. The figure posing against a drum kit with a drumstick in one hand, had smooth, shiny, gelled hair that flopped over one eye, black eye make-up and was wearing a horrible white suit.

"That can't be you?" I asked, shocked.

"I'm afraid so," Dad admitted. "It was my New Romantic period."

"Your what? Oh, never mind. Can I borrow it? Ta!" And I snatched it from his fingers and sped back to the garage.

I arrived to find everyone clustered around the computer, looking very worried. Spex was obviously extremely frustrated.

When I asked, "What's up?" Cookie delivered the worst piece of news yet.

"The computer's broken. We can't print the paper."

Chapter Seven

I felt like crying. Was this the end of everything? If we couldn't get our publicity material together, no one would know about the SOP campaign, and nobody would come. All our hard work would have been for nothing.

"There must be something you can do," I said desperately. "Could you ring a repair man?"

"On Bank Holiday Monday? You must be joking. It would cost a fortune!" Spex scowled at the printer. "Anyway, I don't know if it's the computer or printer that has gone wrong, or if it's a software problem."

I flopped into a chair and covered my face with my hands. Then, suddenly, I sprang to my feet again. "Hey! I think one of Dad's musician friends works for a computer company."

"Then fetch him here pronto!" said Spex.

"Well, I don't know if..."

"Just get him, Tiger!"

I had been going to explain that I didn't know if he was just a salesman, or if he really knew about them and had repair skills, but Spex was too wound up to listen. I just hoped Dad's friends were still there! Luckily they were. Outside our house, the musicians had called a halt to rehearsals and were piling into their various vehicles.

I ran towards them, held up my hand and shouted, "Stop!" just like a traffic policeman.

"What is it?" asked the tall, weedy guitarist.

"Can anyone here mend computers? Ours has broken down. We must get it going again. If we don't, *The Stripes* will never get to play next Saturday!"

Tim, the ginger-bearded bass player, grinned at me. "Let me take a look."

I grabbed his arm and tugged him to the garage, panting in my panic and eagerness.

Tim took one look at our ancient equipment. "You might have warned me that you ran an antiques business," he joked.

Spex explained what seemed to be the matter.

"Why don't you all go and get some lunch and come back later?" suggested Tim. We all agreed, much to the relief of our empty stomachs.

At around half past three, there was a knock on the door and Tim was standing there, with a long face. A gloomy-looking Spex was at his side.

"I can't fix it. The printer's working fine, but the computer's got a hard disk problem," he said. "I'll take it into the shop with me tomorrow and see what can be done."

"But what about the newspaper? And all our publicity stuff?" wailed Spice.

Spex shrugged, and raised his hands in defeat.

"I suppose we could finish some posters and get those put up around town," suggested Sugar. "They won't look very professional as the wording will have to be handwritten, but it's the best we can do..."

"Did you save any of those pages you printed out earlier, with versions of the flyer and the press release on them?" I asked Spex.

"I think so..."

"Well, why don't we photocopy them at the corner shop and take them into Sunnyvale?"

Spex visibly cheered up.

So that was what we did.

While we were in Sunnyvale, it started to pour down with rain.

"Run for it!" I yelled, making for the nearest bit of shelter, which happened to be the doorway of the Internet caff.

As Spex, Spice, Sugar and I stood there, shivering damply — Cookie had stayed at home to clear up her painting things — an incredible thought struck me.

"Spex?" I asked, "Did you save the work you did for the newspaper on floppy disk?"

"Yes, of course. I always do. Why?" He followed my gaze and suddenly, it dawned on him, and he struck his head with his hand. "What an idiot I am! I can print it all out here. That's if they've got a printer I can use..."

We asked. They had. We arrived back at Cosy Crescent soaked to the skin, and Dad kindly offered to run Spex back into town, as Mrs McGee had gone to the hospital in their car. He also said he would wait until Spex had nished, as there would be a lot to carry back. And Dad offered to pay the printing costs, as it was all for a good cause. Good old Dad!

It did mean, though, that I had a hard evening's stapling ahead of me...

*

Jude and Flash returned shortly after five, and called round at my house. Flash was jubilant at having met some of his local football heroes. "Jude took my photo with Kev and Scott. I've got their autographs, too!" he boasted.

"I didn't know you were so keen on football," I said.

"I didn't used to be, but I am now. Maybe I'll be a sports photographer when I'm older!" he said eagerly.

With Flash's excitement I hadn't noticed that Jude was more subdued than normal.

"What's up J?" I asked "Did Mr Queen say it was all right to use the football pitch?" I made a guess at the problem.

"Nope," said Jude miserably. "The reserve team has a match in the afternoon so we can't use it."

"Cheer up," said Flash, positively. "Something will turn up. It has to."

I thought that I would be secretly pleased that the football match was at risk, but I wasn't. I hated seeing Jude so down, and found I really wanted the whole day to be a great success. I racked my brains for a solution, then it came to me.

"Of course! Mrs D.'s field! That's large enough for a football pitch and with loads of room for spectators, don't you think?"

"Well, yes, I suppose so," said Jude. "And it's just about flat enough for a charity fun match like this."

"Well, then, let's go and ask Mrs D. if we can have the match on her eld too. A two o'clock kickoff will tie in nicely with the concert because we want to hold that at ve, so that kids can come along," I reminded him.

Jude grinned. Then he snapped his fingers and whirled round like a dancer, ending up facing me again, slightly breathless. "It's going to be good, I can feel it in my bones!"

"So can I," I said. "I can't wait. We're going to save the pool, I just know it!"

I was in the middle of my evening meal when Spex rapped at the window. He was grinning and brandishing a large, purple stapler! Oh dear... I gulped down my pears and ice cream — yum! — and dashed over to the garage. Mrs Dawkins had willingly agreed to the football match, but my joy was dampened when I saw the huge pile of paper waiting to be stapled. Luckily, Spex had borrowed an extra stapler so three of us made short work of putting together one hundred and fifty copies of the *Sunnyvale Standard*.

"Can everyone help deliver them tomorrow?" Spex asked. We all said yes.

"Leave tomorrow afternoon free. We're having football practice," Jude informed us.

"What? All of us?" Sugar asked, with an appalled expression.

"No, just me, Spex and Flash," Jude said airily.

I thought that was most unfair. Why did it have to be just the boys? I was as good as Spex and much better than Flash, and I told them so. Spice and Cookie wanted to join in, too.

Jude threw up his arms. "OK, OK. We don't need everyone tomorrow, we're just playing five-a-side and we've got enough players with Kev, Scott and their mates. But you can be in the reserve team if you like."

"Huh. That's great!" Spice snorted.

"Well, let's all go, anyway," I said. "But on Saturday we'll be in the main team. Friends United. How about that?"

Cookie loved it, and even Sugar wanted to join in.

By the time the following afternoon came round, we were all exhausted, having tramped around Sunnyvale all morning with backpacks full of *Sunnyvale Standards*, and bags of advertising flyers. Spex hadn't spotted my sneaky addition. The flyers proclaimed the fact that Kev, Scott and Christy

Donovan were playing a celebrity match, but I had added "v. Friends United" in red ink on every one!

I was pleased to see some of our posters on display. Cookie had managed to paint eight, and we had hand-printed the information about next Saturday's events in thick black felt-tip. Dad had taken them into a couple of shops, and they had placed them in their front windows. Our corner shop was also displaying one, and so was the Internet caff. Nobody could miss them, as Cookie's pictures were bright orange and turquoise!

We took copies of the paper and a bunch of flyers into every shop and office in the high street. Then it was time to meet Mr Queen and practise our football skills!

Christy Donovan wasn't there, but Kev and Scott and some of the other Sunnyvale Albion players were. They were all dressed up in crazy clothes — old-fashioned striped swimsuits, wetsuits, snorkels, and Kev was wearing flippers!

"What do you think?" asked Kev. "We thought it would make things more fun on Saturday."

We all said it was a brilliant idea. "Does that mean we'll have to wear *our* swimwear, too?" asked a worried Cookie.

"Why not dress up as a shark?" joked Flash.

Cookie took him seriously. "Oh yes! I'll make myself a big fin!" She loved the idea and none of us wanted to spoil her fun.

We didn't play any serious football, we just looned about and fell over a lot. It was terrific fun. I was really looking forward to Saturday now, even though we still hadn't found the international star whose concert appearance we had advertised. There were still four days to go, though. *Anything* could happen. And, with our luck, it usually did!

Chapter Eight

Wednesday was great fun too. We all got our parents to raid their wardrobes for funny clothes to wear for the football match, then met at Sugar and Spice's house to try things on and have a laugh.

I had a tiny purple, tie-dyed sundress and plimsolls with flowers painted on them, plus one of Mum's mad hats. This one was a bright yellow sombrero, which I had to tie on to the back of my head to stop it from falling down over my eyes.

"Look at this!" squealed Sugar, dancing round in baggy orange shorts and a matching cotton top, both covered in large white polka dots. "Gran says it's called a playsuit and they were all the rage in the 1950s. I can't imagine her in it, can you?"

We all giggled. The playsuit was very small and Granny Hart is very big. But she must have had a good figure fifty years ago!

"Those aren't spots, they're moth holes," laughed Flash.

"Pretty enormous moths, then!" joked Jude.

"You've just got to wear this hat with it," I insisted, tossing her a floppy white cotton hat with an orange felt flower on the front. "Mum got it in a jumble sale. She says it's an original hippy hat from the sixties."

"We're supposed to be wearing beach wear, not giving a historical fashion parade," said Jude, rather impatiently.

"You can talk!" I shot back at him. "That outfit is *so* last year!"

I was only joking, but Jude took me seriously and glared at me. He always liked to be dressed in the latest thing. Although he couldn't afford the expensive brand names, his uncle in America often sent presents over, usually sweatshirts and sports gear, which Jude thought were really cool.

"I've made my shark outfit," said Cookie proudly. "What do you think?" She opened a large plastic bag and brought out an amazing fin made of cardboard,

sprayed with silver paint. It had some elastic attached
to it.

"Put it on!"

"Let's see!"

"Hiya, Jaws!"

Everyone encouraged her, so she pulled the elastic
over her head so that the fin was on her back.

"How about making a shark's head to go with it?"
suggested Spex.

"Because I couldn't see properly and I'd miss the
ball," Cookie pointed out solemnly. "Anyway, if I wear
my silver catsuit that I wore for the school play, I
think I really will look like a shark."

"How about you, Flash?" I asked him. "What are you
wearing?"

"This." He reached into Cookie's bag and produced
a fluorescent pink Hawaiian shirt, patterned with
yellow and green palm trees. "And these." He pulled out
a frilly shower cap and a pair of striped bermuda
shorts. They were all much too big and we all shrieked
with laughter.

"Here's my outfit," said Spex, holding up something
expensive-looking. "It's even older than Grandma
Hart's beach outfit. It belongs to Grandpa. What do
you think?"

"Wow!" I whistled admiringly. "Put it on, Spex!"

He went into the downstairs cloakroom and came out again in immaculate white linen trousers, a matching jacket and a straw boater hat with a striped band round it. Sunglasses completed the effect. He looked like the star of one of those old-fashioned, black-and-white movies that they show on afternoon TV.

Shouts of "Cool!" and "Fantastic!" echoed round the room.

"It's not exactly beach gear..." Sugar commented.

"Let him wear it. It looks great," I said, and Spex grinned and gave me a thumbs-up sign.

"How about you, Sugar?" I said.

She pulled a face. "I haven't thought of anything yet..."

"Oh yes, she has!" yelled her twin.

"Sssh!" Sugar held a finger to her lips. "Don't spoil it. All will be revealed," she added mysteriously.

"OK, that's the costumes sorted. Now, don't you think it's time for Friends United to practise their football skills?" Jude reminded us. "It may be just a fun game, but I'd still like to see us score a few goals."

After we had changed, we took two footballs on to the field and put in some serious practice. We had a great time but it was a jolly good job that Saturday's game was going to be just a fun one, as we certainly wouldn't have been picked to play in the World Cup! We were all really tired that night, so we went back home to take it easy, promising to meet up the following afternoon for more practice, as we all had various boring, parents-connected things to do in the morning.

Thursday was bright and sunny again. There was a real holiday feeling in the air that afternoon as the seven of us headed towards the field.

"I want to be goalie!" Cookie insisted.

"You can't be goalie, you're too short," Sugar pointed out.

"Oh, let her. It doesn't matter who wins," Spex said.

So Cookie went in goal and Jude kicked a series of high shots that sailed high above her head.

"It's not fair! I'm not getting a chance to save anything," she complained, so we banned Jude from kicking the ball for a while, as he's too good, and let Flash take the goal kicks instead.

Round about four o'clock, we were tired and hungry and decided to head for home. When we got back to Cosy Crescent, there a collection of vehicles parked outside my house. Dad's band. It appeared we weren't the only ones who were practising!

I went in to see what was happening and there was our computer on the kitchen table. I ran out again into the front garden. "Hey, Spex! *Spex!*" I yelled in the general direction of the house next door.

There was no response, so I went round and hammered on the door until Spex answered, looking damp and tousled from the shower. "What is it?" he asked, a bit grumpily.

"The computer's back!"

"Has Tim fixed it, then?" Spex asked eagerly.

"Er... I didn't ask," I answered, feeling like a complete idiot.

Spex gave a deep sigh. "Oh, *Tiger!*" he said exasperatedly.

"Sorry. Why don't you come round and ask Tim? Then he'll be able to explain to you what was wrong and how he fixed it."

"*If* it's fixed. OK, I'll be right round."

To our delight, the computer was mended. "Just a little glitch in the software," Tim said. "I've upgraded various programs and added to the memory. It should work much faster now."

"Thanks!" Spex grinned.

"I'll bring it over to the garage for you," Tim offered. "Oh, by the way, I can let you borrow some of the latest scanning software that I'm testing, if you're interested. That would make working with photographs much easier for you."

Spex's smile broadened. "That would be brilliant."

Tim carried the computer over for us and showed Spex the changes he had made. He asked to see something we had been working on, so Spex opened the file containing the ad for the concert.

Tim gazed at it. "Hmm," he said, stroking his beard with his fingernails. "*Mystery International Guest Stars*, eh. Who have you got?"

Spex and I stared at each other glumly, wondering who was going to own up first. In the end, I did.

"No one, yet."

"Oh dear." Tim looked at the pair of us, his blue eyes twinkling. "So it looks as if *The Stripes* are going to be top of the bill! We'd better be good, then!"

I thought of our swimwear parade that morning and a really daft idea came to me. I nudged Spex. "I don't suppose you've got some handy disguises, and can sing in foreign languages? Then you could appear twice," I suggested brightly.

To my surprise, Tim's face went all serious. "You

might have something there, Tiger," he said mysteriously. Then, abruptly, he stood up and strode out of the garage, leaving Spex and me scratching our heads.

"Grown-ups! They're impossible!" he exclaimed. "You never know what they're going to do next."

I completely agreed with him. I had a funny sort of feeling that Tim had something up his sleeve, and I didn't just mean his arm!

Chapter Nine

The main local paper for our area comes out on Fridays, so there was a race to see who would get to the corner shop first, to buy a copy and see if they had given our SOP event a mention. I got there just as Mr Kumar was opening up for business. I waited patiently while he cut the blue plastic tape around the bundle of *Middlesham & District Herald*, which contains a little bit of Sunnyvale news but isn't a patch on our very own *Sunnyvale Standard*!

I handed over the money and was madly flipping through the pages when Spice came in.

"Ooh, let's have a look!" She tried to tweak the paper out of my fingers.

"Get off, it's mine," I told her firmly, but then

took out the middle section and handed it to her.

We took the paper out into the sunshine and sat on the pink front wall of my house to read it. Sugar came racing over, then Spex and Jude saw us and came out, too. I ended up giving everyone a few pages each. However, after much grunting and rustling of pages, we had to admit the depressing truth to ourselves. The paper had given us no publicity at all.

Spex shoved his glasses up his nose with a vicious prod. "Huh!" he exclaimed. "The biggest thing that's happened round here for ages, and they haven't even bothered to mention it. So much for the *Herald*. They wouldn't know big news if it happened outside their window!"

"Oh dear," sighed Sugar and Spice at exactly the same moment.

We saw Mrs Crumble walking towards the shop, with Cookie in tow.

Sugar called out, "Where's Flash?"

"Still in bed," Mrs Crumble replied. "I think he's suffering from lazy-itis this morning."

"He says he bruised his toe on the football," added Cookie.

Jude frowned. "I hope he's still going to play for Friends United," he said. "We can't afford to have anyone drop out."

"Oh, I'm sure he'll be all right," said Mrs Crumble. "Come on, Cookie. You can't have your breakfast till I've bought some milk!"

I felt quite droopy and kicked my heels against the wall. "If nobody knows about tomorrow, that means nobody will come," I said sadly.

"Don't be silly, Tiger," said Jude. "Of course people know about it. How about all those leaflets and copies of the *Standard* that we distributed? And the posters? And Mr Queen and the footballers will have told plenty of people, too."

"Yes, let's stop worrying and concentrate on having a good time," Spex said brightly. "Anyway, I'm still waiting to hear back from Kelly." Kelly worked for our local radio station, *Sunnyvale 6.2*. "I'm sure she's going to do something."

I jumped off the wall and took a deep breath. "Right. Let's have some action round here," I said. "Spex, you can ring Kelly and remind her to mention the event today, not once, but over and over again. On every news bulletin, if possible! Jude, could you ring Mr Queen and see if he has any contacts on the daily papers who might be interested to know that Christy Donovan will be playing football in Sunnyvale tomorrow. Christy has lots of fans around the country. It would be great if they could all come and see him, and put some money into our collection."

"What can *we* do?" asked Spice and Sugar.

I had a think, twisting my hair round my finger in concentration. "I *know!* You can ring all your friends and relatives and make sure they're coming, and tell them to tell all *their* friends, too. And you could ask Flash and Cookie to ring everyone they know as well."

"OK," Sugar agreed. "What about you?"

I glanced at Spex. "I think Spex and I should go into Sunnyvale and check out the response to our leaflets," I said.

We had left heaps of them in high street shops and some in the library, and the Oldies had helped by taking some into various offices and businesses for us. Mrs McGee was even giving them out to patients at the doctors' practice where she worked.

The people we asked said that the leaflets had all gone and people seemed really keen on the idea of helping to save the outdoor pool. Of course, they all wanted to know who the mystery star of the concert was going to be. "That's just the point — it's a mystery!" we told them.

"I'm really worried about letting people down," Spex said gloomily, as we set off for home. "Don't you think we're cheating people, if we say we've got an international star when we haven't?"

"We can always say that their plane was delayed and they couldn't make it..." I shrugged and gave Spex a guilty grin. I felt bad about it, too. "At least people haven't had to buy tickets, so they won't ask for their money back! Anyway..." I added, thinking about what Tim had said, "there's still a chance that someone will turn up at the last minute."

"It very nearly *is* the last minute!" Spex rolled his eyes in a hopeless expression.

The rest of Friday was taken up with last minute preparations — finalising our costumes, collecting jumble, arranging lifts, taking turns to answer people's enquiries on Spex's mobile phone.

Shortly after three, Flash dashed over to my house and said he had just heard Kelly give out the information on the radio after the hourly news bulletin.

"She made it sound really exciting! She said that Christy Donovan would be signing autographs in aid of the Save Our Pool fund and that the mystery international star might be somebody from the pop music charts."

"I'm glad she said 'might be'," I observed. "Otherwise we could be in trouble! I hope Christy *has* agreed to sign autographs..."

"He will. He's a really nice guy," said Flash. "It's going to be incredible, playing on the same football pitch as him tomorrow. I can't wait!"

I was too nervous to eat breakfast the next day. Mum was already setting up her stall outside our house, even though it wouldn't be needed until lunchtime at least! She had decided to sell some of her home-made pots and had been up late last night painting colourful squiggles on them. As I went out to help her, I saw Mr Kumar at the corner shop taking delivery of a large amount of packets of crisps and biscuits and cartons of juice.

Cosy Crescent was a hive of activity. Mr Hart was out, helping put up a big sign Cookie had painted, saying, SAVE OUR POOL! FOOTBALL MATCH THIS WAY, on the corner of Cosy Crescent. Mrs Crumble and Mrs McGee had dragged out all kinds of tables and were piling them with jumble, including lots of games and books that my friends and I had donated, while Holly Hodge, Mr Hart's lodger, was hanging second-hand clothes on a rail. Dad was rigging up a PA system one of his band mates had loaned him.

I waved to Flash, who was kicking a football about with Jude. We all had our orders. Lunch was to be finished by half past one. Then we were all to change into our silly beach clothes for kickoff at two. By then, Cosy Crescent should be crowded with people, all eager to see the footballers, buy things, donate money to our good cause and stay on for the concert at five o'clock

A green Mini painted with racing stripes turned into Cosy Crescent and halted outside my house. I recognised the dark-haired girl who got out of it, carrying a tape recorder and a microphone. It was Kelly, from *Sunnyvale 6.2*.

"Hi, Tiger! Is Spex around?" she enquired after I introduced myself.

"Haven't seen him yet..."

"Well, you'll do. I just need a quick interview about today's events. This is going out in the next bulletin," she explained breathlessly. "Now, introduce yourself and tell me what's happening."

"My name's Tiger Cubb, I'm ten years old and I've helped to organise today's football match and concert, in order to keep Sunnyvale Outdoor Pool open," I began nervously.

Kelly spoke into the microphone. "I understand that football star Christy Donovan will be here," she prompted, and thrust it back towards me.

"Yes, that's right. Kickoff's at two and he'll be signing autographs after the match."

Kelly took over again. "Well, looking round, I can see that it's all happening in Cosy Crescent and everybody is very busy. Lots of stalls are being set up. There's jumble, clothes, home-made goodies, and I hear there's going to be a concert later on, too. Can you tell me who's singing tonight, Tiger?"

My mouth dropped open and I stared blankly at her, in a total panic. "There's my dad's band, *The Stripes*..." I dried up.

"And you've advertised an international superstar. I think it's time we all knew who it's going to be!" Kelly grinned encouragingly, waiting for my reply.

"It's a secret," I blurted.

"Well, at least tell us what country they're from. America? India?"

The microphone was pushed back in my direction again. I just wanted to dig a big hole in the front garden and fall into it! What I didn't know was that my dad had been hovering behind me, listening. He reached out, took the mike and said, "Hi, I'm Jon,

Tiger's dad, and I'm the drummer with *The Stripes*. Let me give you a little clue as to which country tonight's big band is from." He whistled a few bars of the French national anthem, the *Marseillaise*.

Kelly took back the microphone. "Well, there you have it! I hope everyone in Sunnyvale will come down to Cosy Crescent today and join in the fun. It looks as if you'll all have a chance to practise your French tonight, too!"

After Kelly had driven off, I turned to Dad. "How could you?" I exploded. "We haven't got any French musicians. Everyone will call us liars!"

Dad laughed and tapped the side of his nose. "Just you wait and see," he said.

Chapter Ten

Already, by lunchtime, people had started turning up to the SOP event. Families were strolling around, looking at the stalls and buying lots of things. I saw a lady walking off happily with one of Mum's pots, a bright green one with purple flowers on. Cosy Crescent seemed full of the general sound of happy, excited bustling.

Sugar, Spice, Cookie and I all got changed at the twins', as mine was too full of Mum's friends and bits of Dad's drum kit and sound system. Mrs Dawkins was allowing visitors to use her outside loo in the back garden, and a queue was already forming!

Just as Sugar was helping Cookie to fix her shark's fin on, we heard a loud wail from Spice. "Oh no, it's raining!" she cried.

Cookie and I dashed to the window. Sure enough, the sky had darkened and a heavy shower had started. Mr Hart came dashing in for an umbrella, and to find some plastic sheeting to put over Holly's clothes rail.

Then there was a deafening clap of thunder. I looked around at the wan faces of the others. It was just too awful for words. Nobody would want to stand on a soggy field watching a fancy-dress football match in weather like this, no matter how many superstars were playing!

Just as I was sinking into deep despair, I heard cheers ring out in the street, and dashed to the door in time to see a limousine dropping Christy Donovan outside our house. He looked scrummy, and was wearing a scarlet wetsuit and carrying a snorkel! Despite the rain, camera flashes were going off. I could see Flash out there, snapping away, and Mr Kumar was standing outside his shop, doing a roaring trade in cheap umbrellas. Maybe things weren't so bad after all.

I turned to the others. "Come on," I said. "The show must go on!" and I led the way out into the rain.

Two of the Albion players had already checked our

the field and were shaking their heads. All the players were wearing crazy clothes: snorkels, flippers, rubber rings and one even had full scuba-diving gear on — I assumed he'd at least take the air canisters off for the match itself! I saw Jude talking to Kev and Scott, Sunnyvale Albion's biggest stars. Despite the rain, they were laughing and joking. Then Jude called the rest of us over. "We're going to play right here in the crescent," he said. "I've invented a new game. It's called Water Football!"

"What's that?" asked Flash, almost tripping over Kev's flippers in his excitement.

"There's a big puddle at the end of the crescent. Whoever kicks the ball in and makes the biggest splash, has scored a goal," Jude explained. "Points will be deducted for falling over and for kicking the ball into anyone's garden. Grandad's keeping score."

Grandpa McGee, in blue shorts and a green and white striped T-shirt, was standing by the PA under a big umbrella with a notebook and pen.

"Let me tell everybody what's going on," said Christy Donovan talking on the microphone. "Right, everyone!" he announced to the crowd. "Stand well back. Today is a landmark in British football, as we're going to play a brand new game called Water Football, invented by Jude McGee." He explained the rules. "Jude's brother, Spex, is kicking off against Kev Healey. On your marks..."

Grandpa McGee blew a whistle. Spex got the ball and kicked it to me. I quickly passed it to Flash, who gave it a mighty boot which was intercepted by Scott McLeonard. Then Cookie came pelting down the street, grabbed the ball, ran to the puddle and threw it in. It made an enormous splash.

"Goal!" yelled everyone.

"Handball!" called Mrs D. from Number Five, who was wearing a big purple plastic hat to keep off the rain. She obviously hadn't listened to the rules, which included one that the ball could be thrown into the puddle.

"One point to Friends United!" Grandpa McGee decided.

But next time I went after the ball, I tripped over my shoelace and fell over.

"One point deducted from Friends United!" bellowed Grandpa McGee and we all groaned.

But, soon after that, Spice scored, so we were still one up — until Scott got the ball and plunged face down into the puddle with it! Grandpa couldn't decide whether that was a point or not as he had fallen over at the same time!

It was enormous fun and everyone ignored the rain, as they were far too busy cheering and laughing. The game ended in a draw, then Christy, Kev and Scott all signed autographs, in exchange for a donation to our fund. We were collecting all the money in a big plastic dustbin. Sugar had sprayed it silver and Cookie had painted SOP on it in bright red letters. The coins and notes in it were mounting up.

By four o'clock, the rain had stopped. The footballers all stayed on after the game and signed more autographs, while we got things ready for the concert. The stalls had been a great success. All Mum's cakes had been sold and her stall was empty save for one or two pots. Plenty of people had bought toys and jumble, and there were only a few clothes left on Holly's rail.

Mr Hart, who had taken it upon himself to compere our event, stood on a stepladder in the middle of Cosy Crescent with the mike and addressed the crowd.

"I hope you have all enjoyed today's football match in aid of the Save Our Pool fund. I'd like to remind you that the concert will commence shortly, at five o'clock."

My friends and I went indoors to get washed and

changed, leaving people happily milling about outside in the afternoon sunshine, waiting for the concert to start. Dad's band were busy lugging musical gear around. They had spent the afternoon building a makeshift wooden stage in the field, and borrowing loads of fold-up chairs. There was still no sign of anyone French in Cosy Crescent. I hoped Dad hadn't been pulling our legs about it, or we would feel very silly about the radio broadcasting it to all the listeners.

After gobbling down some food I was too nervous to taste, I went next door to talk to Jude and Spex and found them sitting round the dustbin, counting the money. Coins and notes were in piles all over the floor. Spice and Sugar sat eagerly watching them.

"I make it 989.64," said Jude.

"And I make it 1,100.48," insisted Spex.

"It's not..."

"...enough." Spice finished Sugar's sentence. We were used to this by now. They were always coming out with the same thing at the same time, and seemed practically telepathic.

"It's not enough yet, but it's a great start," Spex said optimistically.

"Still, maybe the concert will add a lot more to it," I added brightly.

The door opened and Flash walked in, kicking over a pile of fifty-pence pieces. "Oops, sorry," he said.

"I should think so! I'll have to count them all over again now," Spex muttered.

"I shot off five whole films this afternoon," Flash said proudly. "I used a fast film for the goal splashes, so they should look really great!"

"Dad's got a stage set up and he's put down loads of plastic sheeting so that people won't get their feet too muddy," I told everyone. "I'm really worried, though. Dad won't tell me anything about this French band of his. I don't know if they even exist! What happens if they don't appear?"

"We won't get much money for the fund. That's what will happen," Sugar said.

"I doubt if we've even collected enough to repaint the changing rooms yet," Jude said, with an unhappy sigh.

His mood was beginning to get me down, too. "Let's wait and see what happens," I said, crossing my fingers behind my back.

Five o'clock. the rain had stopped, lots of people had taken their seats and others were still arriving. *The Stripes* were tuning guitars on the stage. Tim, the bass player, lumbered to the microphone, his feet clumping on the wooden boards.

"Lay-*deez* and gentlemen! Allow me to present... *THE STRIPES!*"

Dad gave a thunderous roll on the drums and the band were off, playing for all they were worth. It was great. People got out of their seats and began dancing. The music went on for almost an hour, then Tim announced that there would be a break. "The corner shop is selling drinks and snacks and tea and coffee are available over there." He pointed to a table where Mrs Crumble and Mrs McGee were standing with coffee pots, a large tea urn which they had borrowed from somewhere, and several plates of of biscuits.

"Let's find my dad," I said to Sugar, who was standing next to me.

We went round to the back of the stage and found him standing with Christy Donovan (I think my dad is quite a fan!). "Where are these French people, then?" I asked Dad suspiciously. "And who are they?"

"They're a traditional folk band. Tim and I know them from way back. They've made lots of records in France and they are popular in Canada, too. They were due to leave Brittany this morning, to take the ferry over here. There have been bad weather reports so they may have been delayed. Don't worry. Just in case they don't turn up, we've got these." Dad delved into a box and pulled out some whiskery strips. "False moustaches," he said.

I heard Spice give a loud snort of laughter.

"And these," Dad added, pulling a navy-blue beret and a stripy top out of a sports bag.

"I don't believe it," I said. "Dad, this could be a disaster!"

He winked at me. "It will be fine, Tiger — don't you worry."

I felt a bit queasy. All these people had come here expecting the amazing superstars we had promised and all they were getting was a local band — TWICE! I felt we had let everyone down. I was so preoccupied with negative thoughts that I didn't notice Christy Donovan slip away to make a phone call. I sloped off, defeated, to watch the end of the world's worst concert.

Twenty minutes later, everyone was taking their seats again and there was still no sign of the mythical French musicians. Five men walked on stage and picked up their instruments. Despite their stick-on moustaches and berets, they were still instantly recognisable as *The Stripes*. I could hear people around me starting to mutter, and didn't dare look up.

Suddenly, though, I heard an unfamiliar voice, a female one , singing in French. Amazed, I looked up and saw a striking-looking girl in a long, red dress. It was Holly Hodge, Mr Hart's lodger. Holly was fantastic! You could almost forget it was still *The Stripes* playing — they sounded like a different band. As Holly's song came to an end everyone applauded, cheered and shouted, "Encore!" Holly consulted with the band and then started to sing another.

At least there hadn't been the protests and uproar I had been expecting. I told myself it could have been far worse. As I turned away from the stage to find my friends I came face to face with Christy Donovan.

"Tiger!" he said, smiling. "Just the person I'm looking for. There's someone I'd like you to meet."

I was totally baffled. Who on earth could Christy Donovan, the famous footballer, want *me* to meet? I followed him to the back of the stage where a woman was waiting with her back turned to us. Christy tapped her on the shoulder.

"Tiger, I'd like you to meet my sister, Jazz. She was hoping there might be time for her to sing a couple of numbers tonight."

I was dumbstruck. My mouth had dropped open and I was incapable of shutting it. I was standing in front of Jazz. Jazz! My idol. Every song she released went straight to number one. She was world-famous. And Christy Donovan's sister! Now that I thought about it, I remembered she had a footballer brother.

I was vaguely aware that my friends had all picked up the scent of something exciting and had all clustered around, gawping. I hastily pulled myself together.

"Jazz, it's truly an honour to meet you. Would you really sing something for us?" I stammered.

"I'd be delighted." She replied, grinning. "The only problem is I don't have my backing group with me. Do you think *The Stripes* would mind accompanying me?"

Ha! Did I think they'd mind? Just try stopping them! The others went back to their seats and I waited for the applause to die down after Holly's final number. Just as I was about to go on stage to announce Jazz's arrival, a stranger beat me up there.

A middle-aged man, wearing a long, brown waxed coat and wellingtons stepped up to the microphone.

"If I could just have your attention please, ladies and gentlemen..."

Everyone stopped what they were doing, and stared.

"My name's Philip Godfrey and I am one of the councillors for Sunnyvale."

I glanced at Spex, who was standing nearby. He looked as tense and anxious as I felt.

Muttering had started among the crowd an Mr Godfrey coughed and held up his hand for silence.

"I would just like to say that we have been very touched and moved by the residents of Sunnyvale's support for the pool. Especially the residents of Cosy Crescent, and in particular, the younger ones!" He picked each of us out, naming us all in turn, and asking us to stand up so that people could applaud us. I was amazed. How on earth could he know our names?

Once we had sat down again, he continued: "The upshot is that the council's Leisure Department held an emergency committee meeting this afternoon and, with the support of various local businesses who have also been impressed by what you have achieved, I am pleased to say that Sunnyvale Outdoor Pool is to be modernised and will reopen in July, for all to enjoy."

The cheers that burst out were deafening. Mr Godfrey made his way off the stage and was immediately surrounded by people shaking his hand and slapping his back We pushed our way through the crowd to thank him. "Well done kids," he said. "Without you, the council would never have realised how important the pool was to the people of Sunnyvale."

It was so noisy there was no point trying to announce Jazz. She took matters into her own hands and, after quietly introducing herself to the band, took the microphone in one hand and hid at the corner of the stage.

There was a thunderous drumroll and crash of cymbals. Once again the crowd fell silent and stared up at the stage. From out of the silence came Jazz's unmistakable deep and powerful voice as she belted out her most recent hit *Let's Party*. As she moved into the light at the front of the stage there were huge cheers and yet more clapping. In no time at all there were people dancing everywhere.

My friends and I were jubilant. Cookie was even doing cartwheels and somersaults she was so thrilled. Our two fundraising events had been a storming success. Our minds had already turned to the next issue of the *Sunnyvale Standard*, where we would report the day's exciting events.

"I wonder how Mr Godfrey knew about all this." I remarked to Spice.

"Well you didn't think all our leaflets, posters and

press releases were for nothing did you?" Spex asked, smiling.

Then Flash came running up. "Hey, I've just found out something!" he said importantly. He was looking at Sugar and Spice, rather than me, so I just listened.

"I just heard that Holly Hodge was so surprised at how much people liked her singing she's decided to move to London to try and get a record deal. You know what this means, don't you? Your dad's going to have to find a new lodger!"

"Oh, no!" Sugar and Spice groaned, but I couldn't help laughing because I was so happy. It was great for Holly, we'd all had a fantastic day, and we had saved the pool. It just shows what Friends United can do when they try!

⊙ bang on the door™ ©

friends

Together we make things happen!

Follow the adventures of Spex, Jude, Tiger, Sugar, Spice, Flash and Cookie, as they report on more exciting goings on in their ace newspaper the *Sunnyvale Standard*

FRIENDS

The Friends set up the *Sunnyvale Standard* to fight the plans of a dastardly property developer.

And coming soon...

FRIENDS AGAIN

The Friends discover local animals are in danger and tempers are running high. Can they pull together... and catch the culprit?

An imprint of HarperCollinsPublishers

⊙ bang on the door™ ©

drama queen

Drama Queen makes a drama out of
EVERYTHING. Read about her
latest adventure in . . .

PUPPY LOVE

Drama Queen knows EXACTLY what
she wants, a sweet, cuddly puppy all of her
very own. But her mum and dad are
not impressed! Then her nanny Leo has
an idea . . . But will it put Drama Queen
off dogs for ever?

And coming soon . . .

STAGE STRUCK

 Collins

⚓ An imprint of HarperCollinsPublishers

bang on the door ™ ©

silly billy

Follow the adventures of Silly Billy —
the silliest boy in the WHOLE world.

TIME OUT

Silly Billy has a brand new watch...
But he doesn't quite know how to use it.
When its alarm goes off one hour early
Silly Billy decides to get HIMSELF
ready for school. And that's when the
trouble starts...

And coming soon...

POOL FOOL

An imprint of HarperCollinsPublishers

bang on the door™ ©

poo jokebook
Every pun is guaranteed to pong in this stinky collection!

What do you get if you cross an elephant with a bottle of laxative?
Out of the way!

What do you get if you eat baked beans and onions?
Tear gas!

Packed with wicked whiffs, real stinkers and nasty niffs – jokes that will run and run!

Collins
An imprint of HarperCollinsPublishers

bang on the door™©

Collect 5 tokens and get a free poster!*

All you have to do is collect five funky tokens!
You can snip one from any of these cool Bang on the Door books!

0 00 715209 4

0 00 715309 0

0 00 715212 4

0 00 715210 8

**Send 5 tokens with a completed coupon
to: Bang on the Door Poster Offer**

PO Box 142, Horsham, RH13 5FJ (UK residents)

c/- HarperCollins Publishers (NZ) Ltd,
PO Box 1, Auckland (NZ residents)

c/- HarperCollins Publishers, PO Box 321,
Pymble NSW 2073, Australia
(for Australian residents)

0 00 715220 5

First name: .... Surname: ....

Address: ....

....

....

Postcode: .... Child's date of birth: ...... / .... / ....

email address: ....

Signature of parent/guardian: ....

Tick here if you do not wish to receive further information about children's books ☐

F2

1 token

Terms and Conditions: Proof of sending cannot be considered proof of receipt.
Not redeemable for cash. Please allow 28 days for delivery. Photocopied tokens not accepted.
Offer open to UK, New Zealand and Australia only while stocks last.*rrp £3.99